A Doll for
Marie

To Anne

Also by Louise Fatio and Roger Duvoisin

THE HAPPY LION
THE HAPPY LION ROARS

A Doll for Marie

by Louise Fatio

illustrated by Roger Duvoisin

ALFRED A. KNOPF

NEW YORK

In the city of Paris, there lived a doll
who sighed from morning to night.

She was born long ago, when our great-grandmothers lived.
She wore a handsome dress of faded red silk,
with long lace pantalets that came down to her pretty shoes,
and a plumed hat on her blond curls.
She was indeed a precious antique doll.

But, alas, she was also a very lonely doll.
A long time she had sat in the window of an antique shop,
between a Persian vase and a Chinese teapot,

among antique dishes, clocks, jewels, and snuffboxes.
She stared out toward the street, day after day,
dreaming of little girls, and toy beds, and doll carriages.
"This is no way for a doll to live," she sighed.
"If only I had a little girl to play with.

Oh, to have tea parties and to be read to!"
And she sighed from morning to night.

Yet there lived someone
who loved the doll very dearly,

and that was Marie, the mailman's daughter.

Every day, on her way to school and back,

little Marie pressed her nose against the antique-shop window

to see the dainty doll and to wave to her.

How the doll and Marie wished they could play together!

But Marie was too poor to buy the precious doll,

and, anyway, as everyone knows,

antique dolls are not for little girls to play with.

Sometimes, other little girls came with their mothers and said,

"*Oh, Maman, s'il te plaît.* I want the beautiful doll."

But mothers always said, "Please, do not touch that doll.

It's much too precious for a little girl."

Although the doll would have liked best to belong to Marie,
her heart beat faster every time a little girl walked in.
"Perhaps now is the time . . . ," she hoped.
But no—no little girl ever took her away, ever.

At last, one day, a nice old lady walked into the shop
and admired the doll so much that she bought it at once.
"*Une belle poupée, Madame,*"
said Mr. Bricabrac, the shopkeeper,
as he wrapped the doll in a red box.
The doll was very happy. She was going to a new home,
surely a home with children.

But when the red box was opened in the new home,
the antique doll almost cried.
It was so much like the antique shop!
The same ancient gilded chairs, the same carved tables
covered with antique vases, clocks, trinkets.
There was not a child in the house. That was clear.

The nice old lady sat the precious doll on top of the piano,

between an antique clock and an old candlestick.

"How perfectly charming she looks up there," the old lady said,

and cocked her head to one side, very pleased.

But the doll thought with despair,

"I see that I will spend the rest of my days with antiques."

Now, the old lady had a Siamese cat
who played among the trinkets
and a dachshund who slept on the rug.
The cat looked up at the antique doll with a SUSPICIOUS eye.
With one jump he was on the piano
to spit at the doll and smell her plumed hat.

He gave her a little push with his paw, then another,
and *bang* . . . the doll fell on top of the dachshund
and woke him out of his happy sleep.
"*RRRrrr* . . . ," growled the dachshund, and turned about
to smell the red dress with a SUSPICIOUS nose.

Then he grabbed it and shook it furiously to and fro,

for no reason at all, because puppies *never* do

anything for a reason;

then, seeing that the door was not closed,

he ran out with the doll, down the stairs,

and out onto the sidewalk.

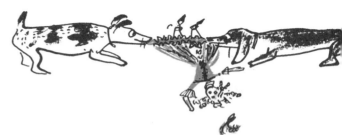

There he met a fox terrier who was looking for a fight.

"*Bow wow wow . . . ,*" barked the terrier.

"What are you doing here with this thing? Give it to me."

He grabbed one end of the red dress
while the dachshund pulled on the other end.
Crack, whiz—the red dress was torn into two pieces,
and the plumed hat rolled into the gutter.

And while the dogs ran off fighting over the dress,
the antique doll lay on the sidewalk in her underwear,
a horrible situation for such a fancy doll.
She was also very bruised and dirty,
and feared the worst was going to happen to her.
But now, guess who should happen to pass by.

Why, little Marie, on her way home from school.

Marie recognized the antique doll and ran to pick her up.

"Oh, *ma belle poupée!*" she cried.

"They did not want you anymore. They threw you away."

She brushed the dust off the doll, kissed her,

and took her home, holding her tight against her heart.

Marie sewed new underwear for the doll,
a cotton dress, and a pair of slacks for
cold weather.

Every day, when Marie came home from school, she said,
"Let's have tea."
Then they read together from their favorite books—
stories of dolls, of fairies, and of animals.

And the doll sighed no more.
She had a little girl to love her,
to kiss her good night and tuck her into bed.
She was no longer a fancy doll, to be sure,
but who cared to be a precious antique doll . . .
if one is not loved?

THIS IS A BORZOI BOOK PUBLISHED BY ALFRED A. KNOPF

Visit us on the Web! randomhouse.com/kids

Educators and librarians, for a variety of teaching tools, visit us at RHTeachersLibrarians.com

Library of Congress Cataloging-in-Publication Data
Fatio, Louise.
A doll for Marie / Louise Fatio, Roger Duvoisin.
p. cm.
"Originally published by McGraw-Hill, New York, in 1957."—Copyright page
Summary: A fancy china doll hopes to find a home.
ISBN 978-0-385-75596-2 (trade) — ISBN 978-0-385-75597-9 (lib. bdg.) — ISBN 978-0-385-75598-6 (ebook)
[1. Dolls—Fiction.] I. Duvoisin, Roger, 1904–1980, illustrator. II. Title.
PZ7.F268Do 2015 [E]—dc23 2014003766

The text of this book is set in 16-point Adobe Jenson Pro.

MANUFACTURED IN CHINA
March 2015
10 9 8 7 6 5 4 3 2 1
First Alfred A. Knopf Edition